BEWARE THE SNAKE'S VENOM

CHOOSE YOUR OWN

NIGHTMARE... #2

BEWARE THE SNAKE'S VENOM
BY KEN McMURTRY

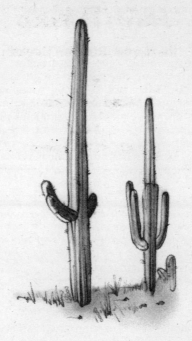

ILLUSTRATED BY BILL SCHMIDT

An R. A. Montgomery Book

BANTAM BOOKS
NEW YORK · TORONTO · LONDON · SYDNEY · AUCKLAND

RL 4, age 008-012

BEWARE THE SNAKE'S VENOM
A Bantam Book/June 1995

CHOOSE YOUR OWN NIGHTMARE™ is a trademark of
Bantam Doubleday Dell Books for Young Readers,
a division of Bantam Doubleday Dell Publishing Group, Inc.
Registered in U.S. Patent and Trademark Office and elsewhere.

Cover and interior illustrations by Bill Schmidt
Cover and interior design by Beverly Leung

ISBN 0-553-48230-0

Published simultaneously in the United States and Canada

Bantam Books are published by Bantam Books, a division of
Bantam Doubleday Dell Publishing Group, Inc. Its trademark,
consisting of the words "Bantam Books" and the portrayal of a
rooster, is Registered in U.S. Patent and Trademark Office and in
other countries. Marca Registrada. Bantam Books, 1540 Broadway,
New York, New York 10036.

PRINTED IN THE UNITED STATES OF AMERICA

OPM   0 9 8 7 6 5 4 3 2 1

To Christopher
and his scary friends the Cooks:
Jody, Bruce, Casey, and Dean.

You have probably read books where scary things happen to people. Well, in *Choose Your Own Nightmare,* you're right in the middle of the action. The scary things are happening to you!

Finding a treasure in the desert won't be easy. Especially in *this* desert. It's haunted!

Fortunately, while you're reading along, you'll have chances to decide what to do. Whenever you make a decision, turn to the page shown. The thrills and chills that happen to you next will depend on your choices.

So make sure you choose carefully—or else your first treasure hunt may be your last.

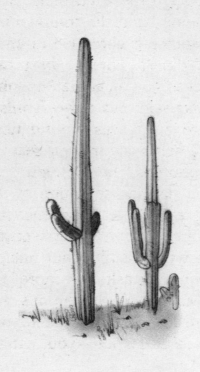

"How much farther to Uncle Evan's?" you ask.

"The archaeological dig is near the base of the White Mountains," says your driver, pointing through the windshield of the Jeep. It's almost dusk, and the mountain range in the near distance is shrouded in an ominous cloud of darkness. For the past two hours since he picked you up at the Phoenix airport, the driver has said only a few words.

"Are there any caves around here?" you ask, shifting nervously in your seat.

"Yeah. Hundreds," he tells you.

You feel a nagging sensation of dread, remembering your cave experience last summer. You hope you don't have to go anywhere near a cave while visiting your uncle Evan.

Before you can ask any more questions, you arrive at the dig. It reminds you of an Indiana Jones movie! You feel your pulse quicken in anticipation—you can't believe you're here!

Turn to page 2.

2

You've always been fascinated by archaeology—especially petroglyphs, which are drawings on rocks. The only ones you've ever seen are in books—not counting the time you visited the Metropolitan Museum in New York. But you've heard that there might be some kind of Native American petroglyphs here in the desert.

As the car comes to a stop, your stomach feels queasy, and your hands tingle. Your interest in archaeology is what brought you here. But something almost kept you away—your cousin Maggie. There she is, standing near one of the tents, waiting for you. It's the first time you've seen her in a whole year.

Last summer you and your family went on vacation to Granite Caverns with Uncle Evan and Maggie. One day you went exploring on your own and managed to get stuck in a cave. A park employee had to get you out, and you were totally embarrassed. Maggie couldn't stop teasing you about it. As usual, she acted like a know-it-all about the whole thing.

Go on to the next page.

Even though you two are the same age, she always acts as if she is much older. She is so sure of herself that it makes you sick. You see her blond hair blowing in the wind. She looks taller than ever, and her teeth are white and straight.

"Hey," she says, taking your backpack from you as you hop out of the car. "What's in here? A bag of rocks?"

"Hi to you too," you say. "It's just some books on petroglyphs."

"Well, you won't have time for books here. Dad will keep you too busy." She gives you a fake-sweet smile. "Besides, if you have any free time you'll probably want to go cave exploring."

"Very funny," you snap. You should have known she wouldn't forget. You change the subject. "How are things going?" you ask, pointing to a group of workers near the edge of a roped-off site.

"Pretty good," she says slowly. "But some strange things have been going on around here."

"What do you mean?"

Turn to page 4.

4

"I'll tell you later. Come on." She leads you toward the site. Your heart pounds with excitement. The workers have uncovered some ancient artifacts. A few people are working on dislodging what looks like an old pot from the earth, while others are busy taking notes and examining other artifacts.

"Wow!" you exclaim. "This is terrific!"

"The ropes are up so no one will step into the excavation," Maggie says as she heads toward a large tent. Several people are sitting around tables. "Yesterday we found some silver charms—and bones."

"Charms?"

"You really don't know anything," Maggie says. "The ancient tribes buried their dead with charms to help them on their way in the afterlife. Otherwise they would be stuck here on earth as ghosts."

"Ghosts?" you repeat. "Why would they be stuck here?"

"To protect the sacred burial grounds from intruders," Maggie says, giving you a serious look.

"Intruders? Like archaeologists?"

Go on to the next page.

"Very funny," says Maggie, rolling her eyes. "Of course we're not intruders. My dad has a special grant from the university."

"You haven't seen any, have you?" you ask.

"What, archaeologists?"

"No, ghosts."

Maggie shrugs. "I've heard them," she says. "Every night this past week they've moaned and made noises like they were coming out of the mountains to get us. It gives me the creeps."

"It's about time!" bellows a familiar voice. You turn and see a large patch of tan shirt just before Uncle Evan wraps you in his big bear-like arms. His beard is rough against your shoulder and he smells faintly of dust, pipe tobacco, and sweat. "Let me look at you," he says.

As your uncle steps back you see the twinkle in his pale blue eyes and the food stains on his shirt. He is big and round, curious and friendly, and loves to play practical jokes. He's also very smart—he's a college professor and leader of this archaeological project. "I hope you're ready for a fun summer," he says.

Turn to page 6.

You laugh. "You mean a summer of work!"

"Work is fun," he says, chuckling. "Stow your things away and then come have dinner with us."

"You've been hearing ghost noises for the past week?" you ask as Maggie shows you to your tent.

"That's right," she says. "And a lot of strange things have been happening as well."

"Like what?"

"Things have been disappearing. Like food from the cook's tent. And someone took stuff from Dad's safe."

"Did he tell the police?"

"Sure, but they didn't think a few pounds of beef jerky, twenty-two dollars, and an Indian clay pot were important enough to issue an all-points bulletin," Maggie says with a shrug.

"What about the sounds at night?"

Maggie smiles. "My dad didn't mention the sounds to the sheriff. But that would be a good project for us this summer, don't you think? Ghost hunters."

Turn to page 31.

Almost ten minutes have gone by. You decide to see what Lisa's up to. Maybe you can talk her into buying some potato chips. You walk to the back—and Lisa is nowhere in sight. Then you see her. She's on a pay phone, whispering to someone on the other end.

"Yes. A Ghost Dancer stone. This one looked liked the real thing," you hear her say.

As she hangs up, you give a loud cough.

"Oh!" she says, startled. "I was just calling the, uh, weather line. To see what the forecast is."

"Mmmm," you say. Why is Lisa lying? And who was she telling about your stone?

You wait while Lisa pays for the supplies, then head back for the Jeep.

"Penny for your thoughts," Lisa says, looking at you.

You swallow. "Nothing much. Just thinking how dry and empty the desert is." Lisa is looking at you kind of funny—like she knows that you know she lied. You feel nervous—and ready to get back to the dig and Uncle Evan.

Turn to page 50.

8

You look around. "I don't think anything's missing. I don't have anything that could be considered valuable."

"Well it beats me what it was," your uncle says, scratching his head. "There's an old miner, Casey McKee, who lives up in the mountains. I think he's been helping himself to some of the kitchen supplies while we're sleeping. He's one of those treasure hunters we were talking about at dinner. He seems harmless. I don't think he'd come into your tent." His voice trails off. "Maybe it was an animal. Sometimes they get into tents if the flaps aren't zipped."

"I'm going back to bed," Maggie says. "It was only a dream."

"Try to get some sleep," your uncle tells you. "You're safe now."

Turn to page 74.

You can't leave Lisa like this. You rig a makeshift shade out of canvas, then crouch at Lisa's feet. Trying to stay calm, you sit and wait.

Lisa's breathing is labored, a series of shallow gasps. It takes you a minute to find her erratic pulse. The vultures keep their distance, circling and waiting.

The sound of a loud muffler startles you. In the distance you see a banged-up old Jeep, throwing off a cloud of dust, heading your way.

You jump up and down and wave your arms. "Help us!" you yell.

The Jeep clanks to a stop and an old man with a head that resembles a sun-baked tomato steps down from the car. "By whompers, I've found a kid. This is a great day indeed. Let me show you my cut. See?" The old man holds out a leathery brown arm that looks perfectly fine to you.

This man must be crazy, you think. But you don't have a choice. "Could you help us?" you ask. "We ran out of gas, and my friend Lisa passed out from heatstroke. She needs to be taken to a hospital. Fast!"

Turn to page 49.

10

Maggie has a huge grin on her face. She's staring at the cave—but then she turns to face you. "If it can glow, it can be cursed," she says in her practical way. "Maybe you'd better go back to the dig. I don't want you to start crying or anything. Based on your past experience, of course."

"Ha ha ha. Very funny," you say. "Can't you just forget last summer?"

Maggie nods. "Yes. I should be able to forget it," she tells you in a serious voice. "If only I could get the picture of you wedged in that cave opening, your feet kicking back and forth in those old sneakers of yours, out of my mind." She breaks off, laughing so hard she's almost crying.

You are really mad. "Look. I've had just about enough. *I'm* the one with the stone, smarty-pants. You can stand out here all day for all I care. I'm going after the treasure myself." Throwing the map at her, you walk briskly into the cave. As you enter, you hear a scuttling sound near your feet. Then silence.

Turn to page 84.

"Not just any rock," you hiss. "This one has petroglyphs on it. It looks very old."

"Can I see it?" asks Maggie.

"Sure, I guess." You reach into your pocket and take it out.

"It's beautiful," Maggie says. "Look at the little pictures. This must have taken a lot of time and patience to make."

"Do you think it's a genuine artifact?"

"It looks genuine to me," Maggie says.

"I should let Uncle Evan take a look," you say.

"Wait a minute," Maggie says, pulling at your sleeve. "Maybe we can figure out what it means. The treasure of Teewah and Nila is hidden in these mountains. This could be a clue. If we could find the treasure of the White Mountains, we'd be famous!"

"People have been looking for it for years. What makes you think we can find it?"

"This, stupid." Maggie holds up your stone. "The legend is that *he who finds the treasure is talked to by a stone.*"

Turn to page 21.

Finally you can't stand it. *"Help!"* you find yourself screaming. Your eyes wide with fear, you stare blindly into the darkness, clutching your blanket. The intruder has disappeared! Then, without warning, a bat flashes past your head, swooping in frantic, tight circles around your cot, all the while screeching as if wounded. Then it is gone.

"Are you all right?" Your uncle Evan bursts into your tent wearing his boxer shorts and a worn pair of jogging shoes. He is holding a flashlight in his left hand and a hammer in his right.

"Something was in my tent!" you shout as Maggie pokes her head in.

"What? Where?" Uncle Evan says, looking around.

"Just now," you say. "A shadow. It was messing around with my things and when I screamed it turned into a bat and . . . and . . . it disappeared."

"You were dreaming," Maggie yawns.

"No," you say firmly. "It's true. Whatever it was disappeared after I screamed for help."

Turn to page 62.

14

On the floor, in a small alcove, is a pair of human skeletons. Silver bracelets circle the arm and anklebones. An eagle feather rests near the skull of one, and near the other, two timeworn pieces of hair ribbon. "Those must be the bones of Teewah and Nila," you whisper.

Then you notice some more cave drawings. "More petroglyphs," you say. "They must hold the key to the treasure!" Eagerly you try to figure them out.

"What are you doing?" shrieks Maggie. "Don't you hear the footsteps? Coyote is going to kill us—just like he probably killed Casey McKee!" She looks frantically around the room. "We've got to hide!"

*If you and Maggie hide,
turn to page 22.*

*If you keep on trying to translate the drawings,
turn to page 65.*

Coyote looks up from his plate. "A magician," he says.

Your uncle laughs. "He doesn't do tricks like David Copperfield. He's a medicine man, a healer, a sage, a storyteller. Coyote knows the ways of the Apaches and can give us advice about how to handle delicate aspects of the dig without violating tribal customs."

"Evan speaks of me as though I have supernatural power." Coyote grins. "So be careful."

Maggie, who has been working on ignoring you, comes over to the table. "What did you find today? Anything special?"

"Maybe—we really won't know until we clean everything off," says a female voice. A young woman wearing a T-shirt and khaki pants sits down next to Coyote. Her complexion is deep bronze from the sun, and her red hair is pulled back into a loose ponytail.

"I'm Lisa," she says, offering you her hand. "Chief cook and bottle washer, as well as graduate archaeology student." She nudges Coyote. "Did you tell our visitor about the legend?"

Your ears perk up. "Legend? About what?"

Turn to page 27.

She shrugs. "If you'll let me keep the whole treasure."

"Ha!" you say, screwing the cap back on the canteen. You hike over to the cliffs. It's kind of rocky, and tumbleweed blows in clumps around your feet.

"Hey! There!" Maggie cries, dropping her map and running over to the cliffs.

You stoop to pick up the map, and when you stand up, you see that Maggie has stopped outside the cave.

"What's the matter, harebrain?" you call out, feeling brave. "Too scared to go in?" You jog over to where she stands and stop in your tracks. It's definitely the mouth to a cave. And outside it sits a ceramic urn. Around it lies a small pile of bones. Human bones.

"Whoa!" Maggie says, looking at the bones.

"These belonged to a person!" you whisper. You want to get a closer look, but you're kind of nervous.

"No duh," says Maggie, rolling her eyes. "My dad and the other archaeologists have found several human bones. Just not so many in one place."

Turn to page 75.

Soon you're forced to crouch down. All the fears of the previous summer flood your memory—the trip with your family and Uncle Evan and Maggie to Granite Caverns that almost claimed your life. You were lost then as you are now. And once again, you are forced to crawl on your belly through a narrow, low, dark, wet passageway. It almost makes you pass out.

"I have to be strong," you tell yourself, trying to stay calm as you crawl. "It's the treasure of a lifetime! And Maggie will be furious."

Scrape. The ceiling of the cave has just scraped your head. The opening becomes narrower and smaller, until the cave ceiling touches your back. You blow the air out of your lungs and inch further into the narrow passage, focusing on the light of the stone in your hand.

Maybe you should turn around now. It hurts to breathe. You begin to push with your hands, trying to back out, but you are wedged in the opening. Your legs and feet scrape against the cave floor, but you don't move an inch.

Turn to page 87.

18

In the distance you can see Spider Rock, a needle formation. You see by the map that it's very near the outpost.

Using an old piece of canvas, you erect a makeshift tent to shade Lisa. The sun is directly overhead as you set off across the shimmering desert terrain in the direction of the needle rock. The sand slows you down, and after an hour of walking, each step is an act of willpower. Sweat has soaked through your T-shirt, and your tongue is so dry it feels like a leather flap in your mouth. When you swallow, it's as if your throat is being raked by broken glass.

What you wouldn't give for a nice cool glass of water, you think. You look back toward the Jeep. It's a tiny speck. You wipe the sweat off your face and keep going. Then, in the distance, you see someone!

"Hey!" you yell. But your voice is feeble and weak, and you know the person hasn't heard you. Your feet feel as if they have fifty-pound weights on them as you try to run.

Turn to page 67.

"That looks like a Ghost Dancer stone," Lisa says, looking interested.

"What's that?" you ask as the Jeep bumps over the rocky terrain.

"Ghost Dancer was a warrior long ago. There are hundreds of stories about him. Some are about his being a shape-changer, but most are connected with the Teewah and Nila legend."

The road follows the contour of a mountain. The hillside is blanketed with blooming purple cactus. Long, delicate needles reach out from beneath the blooms. It's getting hot. You're glad you wore your baseball hat today.

"So this is a picture of Ghost Dancer on the stone?"

"Yes. He protects the bones of Teewah and Nila from treasure hunters until the sacred stone is returned to the tribe," Lisa tells you. "Until then, their spirits cannot journey to the afterworld."

Turn to page 37.

20

"Let us begin," Coyote announces. "Please. We must have total concentration." He tells you all to close your eyes and hold hands. Then he begins to chant. You repeat after him. Then you all raise your hands in the air and return them to your laps. Slowly you open one eye. Everyone is calm and still. Coyote sits in the middle, near a large campfire, his arms upraised.

This is ridiculous, you think. You can't believe you agreed to do this. You'd much rather be thinking about some good books you've just finished—or that great movie you saw last month.

If you decide to just pretend to be listening to Coyote and think about other things, turn to page 73.

If you really go along with the séance, turn to page 88.

"That's a riddle," you say.

"But maybe this stone can talk to us if we can figure out what it says. Come on, it will be our secret. Don't be a fraidycat."

"I'm not a fraidycat," you say angrily. You feel your face turning red. Maggie has no right saying you're afraid. You're about to tell her this when someone taps you on the shoulder.

"Hello," says a deep voice. Startled, you drop a piece of bacon. It's Coyote.

"What's that I see you have?" he asks, bending toward you. Maggie shoots you a warning look. "I hope you haven't been messing around with the site," he says, sounding annoyed.

Turn to page 66.

22

Maggie darts behind a large statue—and you decide you'd better hide too. You crouch down behind a pottery urn, hold your breath, and wait.

Footsteps sound heavily in the tunnel outside.

"Hello! Is anyone in there?" Coyote calls out.

You're startled to hear Maggie speak up. "This is the ghost of Nila. Stay away from this room." *Why doesn't she just keep quiet?* you think nervously. This is no time for games. It's funny, though—Maggie's hiding behind a large statue in the corner, but the voice sounds like it's coming from the middle of the room.

Suddenly you are startled by another voice. "Why have you disturbed us?!" This one sounds like a man. And Maggie's voice is high-pitched. You and Maggie slowly creep out from your hiding places. There, in front of the bones, are the ghosts of Teewah and Nila! And they look very, very angry.

Turn to page 35.

"I guess I'll stay here," you tell Lisa. "I'm kind of anxious to check things out."

"Sure. Another day," she says, getting up to make more coffee. Maggie comes over and sits down beside you with a tray of bacon, toast, scrambled eggs, and orange juice. "Any more boogeymen creep into your tent last night?"

"You can joke," you say, "but something strange is going on."

"What do you mean?" She gives you a serious look.

"Well, I know someone—or something—was inside my tent last night. I have proof."

"What, did you find bat droppings?" Maggie throws back her head and laughs.

"Maybe you're not interested."

"I'm interested," Maggie says. "Can't you take a joke?"

Looking around, you lower your voice. "I found a rock on the ground."

"Hmm," Maggie whispers. "A rock in the desert. Very strange. Yes, very strange. Don't tell anyone."

Turn to page 11.

24

Coyote gives you goose bumps. You suspect that he has a special interest in this stone. "We don't have anything at all," you lie.

"We're just fooling around," Maggie adds. "This is all we have." She holds out a marble she had in her pocket to Uncle Evan. "See, Dad? That's it."

"No. I know I saw—" Whatever Coyote is about to say is interrupted by the sound of workers climbing out of the excavation.

Seizing the opportunity, you and Maggie scramble off your seats. "See ya!" you cry, as you run off to her tent. Maggie fumbles around with some books until she finds what she is looking for—a worn old map of the White Mountain Range. She stabs her finger at a spot on the map. "Here's where we're going. This is where I think the cave is."

Turn to page 56.

"We're not really driving into town," Lisa explains as you hop into the Jeep. "It's more like an outpost."

"Outpost?"

"A small shop that sells supplies," she says. "It's near the highway. Much closer than driving to town." As she talks, you take the stone out of your pocket. It feels warm, almost as if it were alive.

"I found this in my tent last night," you say, fingering the stone.

Turn to page 19.

26

You take Maggie's hand with your free one and rush back the way you came. Near the narrow section of the cave, the stone fades completely. This is the first time in your life that you have experienced total darkness. It is not a great experience.

You feel your way along the wet, slimy walls. Behind you you hear a clacking sound accompanied by chanting and drumming.

"Hurry," Maggie says. "It feels like the cave is going to swallow us."

"We'll get out of here. Keep calm." You hope Maggie takes your advice because your own heart is keeping time with the ghostly tom-tom, and the sound is getting closer.

Maggie's yelp is right in your ear. "Something tried to grab me!"

You see the entrance now, a low gray light. "Almost there," you pant. "Keep running."

With a last burst of energy the two of you rush out of the cave. An angry rumbling sound erupts behind you. You turn and look into the mouth of the cave.

Turn to page 76.

"Ah, Teewah and Nila. A very sad tale," Coyote says. He straightens his back. "Many, many years ago," he begins, "despite their families' warnings, a young Indian man named Teewah, and a young woman, Nila, fell in love. They were from different warring tribes. They met secretly in a cave and planned to run away together. One afternoon, Nila's brother grew suspicious. Nila had worn her finest clothing and had laced her hair with beautiful blue and gold ribbons just to go for a walk. He followed her and discovered the secret meeting place.

"Then he waited, and as soon as Nila left he killed Teewah. The legends say he stung Teewah's heart with the fangs of a rattler and then used his knife to carve the image of the snake on Teewah's chest."

"He used a rattlesnake to kill him?" you ask.

"Yes," Coyote says. "Nila's tribe were snake people. They communed with the snakes and could handle them without fear."

Turn to page 52.

"No sir," you say shakily. "Our car broke down."

You seem to be heading in the direction of the outpost. In the distance you can see some small buildings.

"Looky there." The old man points at something on the side of the road. "Every time I pass by here those two young Indians try to catch a ride. I'm too smart for them, though. Like I said, there's no way I'm givin' rides to hitchhikers."

You stare out into the desert. Fifty yards from the side of the highway is an Indian couple. They are dressed in modern clothes and as you pass by they wave to you. Something about them feels familiar.

You look back. This time the young man is wearing a buckskin outfit and moccasins. On his chest is a long, snakelike scar that starts at his heart and ends near his side. The young woman's beauty is breathtaking. And in her long black hair, she wears beautiful blue ribbons.

The End

"Oh, forget her!" you say angrily to yourself. You had plenty to drink this morning, so you should be okay. And you remember how to get back to the dig. You feel along the wall until you come to a break. You decide to turn right and continue moving cautiously, listening all the time for strange noises.

Swish. You stop. Swish. There's that sound again. Behind you. Faint, but you still hear it. A kind of leathery flapping from time to time. A wind movement. There is something down here with you. Quickening your pace, you move on like a blind person, feeling your way around each turn.

Suddenly you feel a solid wall in front of you. You must move to the right or left. Remembering your stone, you hold it up first in one direction, and then the other. It glows brightly when you hold it to the left.

Swish. You hear the noise again.

"Maggie?" you call out. You're determined to get to the treasure before she does. Quickly you move forward through the tunnel. But it seems as if it's getting smaller with every step you take.

Turn to page 17.

"Get real," you say.

After you stow your things, you and Maggie join your uncle at the mess tent. Uncle Evan introduces you to everyone. He tells them of your interest in rock drawings—and that you're handy with a shovel.

"Hi," you say as you sit down.

The man sitting across from you at the table smiles. His face is lean and dark and as wrinkled as a walnut.

"This is my native guide and assistant project director, Peter Coyote," Uncle Evan says.

"Coyote is an interesting name," you say, helping yourself to some beef stew.

"He's an Apache shaman," your uncle says. "A very wise man."

"What's a shaman?"

Turn to page 15.

You try to ignore her. Suddenly the wind begins to pick up and you can hear a strange whistling sound.

"Must be the wind passing over the rocks," you say.

"Yeah, I guess," Maggie says. The two of you follow a narrow trail up the stony surface of the mountain. It winds around in a spiral.

"Do you think we're getting anywhere?" asks Maggie, taking a swig from the canteen.

You hold up the stone for Maggie to see. "Look. It's getting warm—and it's starting to glow."

"That reminds me of your face after they pulled you out of the Granite Caverns. Warm —and glowing!" Maggie says, laughing.

You ignore her. "I think the stone will lead us to the treasure," you say.

The trail has narrowed. You can look almost straight down into the valley below. Without warning Maggie jumps forward, bumping into you hard, almost knocking you down. A deep rumbling sound seems to come from inside the mountain, and you feel a trembling, as if the mountain's alive.

Turn to page 42.

Quickly you shove the stone under your pillow. Maybe if you ignore the noises, they'll go away. But no. They're getting louder and louder. Suddenly your tent begins to shake! It must be the evil spirits that Lisa was talking about! The séance worked—and now the spirits are coming after you.

Then you have a horrible thought. What if Maggie was right? What if there is some kind of spider woman outside, ready to snare you in her web?

"Help!" you cry, praying that someone will hear you. *"Help!"* You huddle underneath your sleeping bag.

"My web is waiting," groans a low voice. Cringing, you hear the tent flap open. Footsteps shuffle across the ground.

Turn to page 51.

34

The wind whistles through the cave, sending a chill through your body. You hear the sound of flapping wings deep in the tunnel. You and Maggie move forward into the darkness.

"Wait. I can't see!"

"Shhh, I'm right here. Listen," you tell her.

The air around you comes alive, and you feel something swoop past your head. Turning, you move back toward Maggie. She is bent over, holding her hands over her head. A black cloud of bats streams around her. She screams. You grab her hand and pull her forward out of the path of the bats.

"One's in my hair!" she shrieks.

"No, they're gone," you say, trying to calm her down. "Really."

Maggie wipes a tear from her face.

"Okay. Let's stay calm and keep moving," you coax, trying to sound brave. Then, in the distance, you hear footsteps. They sound like they're coming from deep within the cave. Maggie stops moving, her back against the wall, staring at you. "Do you hear that?" she asks.

Turn to page 39.

"Help!" screams Maggie, hiding behind you.

"Coyote!" you cry. "We're in here. With ghosts!" But there's no answer. Outside, you hear Coyote laugh.

"Kids," he says. "That Maggie is such a joker. That's what I get for walking all the way out here to give them an extra canteen of water." You hear the canteen drop. "It's out here if you and the ghosts get thirsty!" he calls in to you. Then you hear his footsteps fade.

You look at Maggie, then back at the ghosts. They're coming closer.

"We'll leave if you open the door," you say.

"That—that's right," Maggie stammers. "We didn't mean any harm. Just let us out."

The ghosts smile. You sigh with relief.

Then Nila speaks up. "You're not going . . . anywhere!"

The End

"It'll be fun," says Lisa, pulling your arm.

"All right," you say reluctantly, tucking the stone under your pillow. You follow her outside, where all the workers—including Maggie —are seated in a circle.

"Hi fraidycat," Maggie whispers as you sit down next to her. "I didn't think you'd have the guts."

"Where's Uncle Evan?" you ask, looking around.

"He had to drive those reporters back to Phoenix. The road is pretty twisty if you're not familiar with it. He'll be back soon."

The night air is cool and very dark. You don't see any stars in the sky. Everyone is talking in hushed whispers. You can tell that some people are nervous, especially when the long howl of a wild dog breaks the silence.

Turn to page 20.

"What happened to the sacred stone?" you ask.

"Nila's brother, the one who killed Teewah, was banished from the tribe as his punishment. Before leaving, he stole a sacred stone from the tribal shaman."

"And Ghost Dancer?"

"He was chosen to guard the place of Teewah and Nila's death until the stone is returned."

You hold out your hand. "This stone."

"If it's the real thing," Lisa says, smiling. "There are a lot of fakes around. I wouldn't worry though, since no one has found the cave where they died."

Turn to page 45.

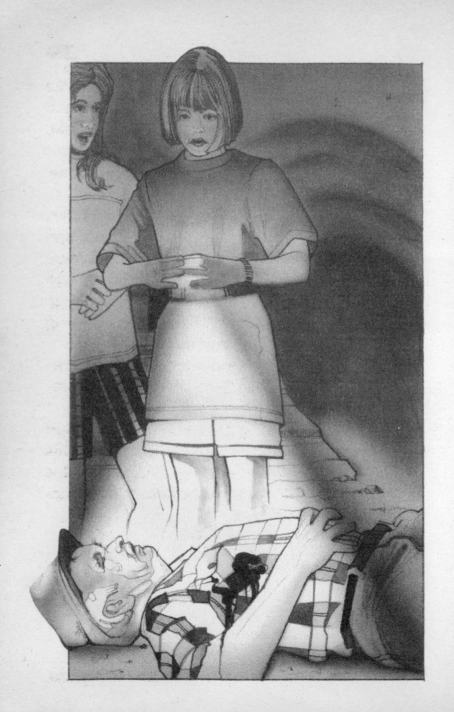

"Come on," you say. "Run this way!" As you run, the stone becomes brighter and brighter. You must be getting close to the room.

"Don't leave me," Maggie says. You know she's scared too.

You hurry. Your feet pound the cave floor, moving as fast as they can. The light from the stone helps you find your way. *Uff!* Something is lying across the tunnel path, and you trip right over it, Maggie on your heels. Shaking, you hold the stone up. There's a body lying there!

"Ahhhhh!" you scream, scrambling backward. Maggie is speechless with terror. Trembling, she points at the body.

It's a man, wearing a tattered plaid shirt and a dirty old cap. Dried blood is caked on his shirt pocket—where a bullet has pierced his chest. "Casey!" Maggie shrieks. "Casey Mc-Kee's been murdered!"

Turn to page 60.

40

"No, I'm tired. Good night," you say, hoping Lisa will leave.

"Okay. Suit yourself," she says. Is it your imagination—or does she look mad? You shake your head and put the stone on your bed. Then you open one of your petroglyph books.

After an hour, you put the book down. You've learned a lot about markings, but nothing that will help you now. Yawning, you take a bite of a granola bar.

While you were reading, the constant whining of a tiny generator filled the night air. But now you hear another noise. It sounds like someone crying. The wind shakes the canvas of your tent with sudden gusto, and you look up from your book, startled.

There is something outside—a noise, a scratching sound at your tent flap. Uneasily, you think of last night. It wasn't a dream. You're sure of it.

Turn to page 33.

But you have no plans to attend the séance. After a late lunch, you wander around. Your stone is safe in your pocket. Some reporters from Phoenix have driven out to look at the dig, and Uncle Evan has offered to take them on a tour. You decide to join them.

"Welcome to Section C," says Uncle Evan, as you head over to the tents where most of the action has been taking place. "This is where we keep all the artifacts we've unearthed. We've even reconstructed what appears to be an ancient altar."

"All those who walk here, beware," says a deep voice in your ear.

"Beware?" you say, jumping in alarm. It's Maggie.

"Of ghosts and goblins and things that go bump in the desert!" Maggie laughs.

Coyote steps forward. "This is a sacred place," he says. "Jokes should not be made. Or else . . ."

"You are quite right," Uncle Evan says. "The remains of ancient civilizations deserve our respect."

Turn to page 59.

42

"Why couldn't Teewah and Nila have met in a nice quiet place?" you say. "Like a café. At sea level."

As you near the top of the mountain, you come across the mouth of a small cave. The entrance is narrow, and a lone cactus sits to the left of it.

You hold the stone up in front of the cave entrance. It glows as bright as a lamp. "This must be it! We must be getting really close to the treasure!" you say excitedly. "Look at the stone!"

Turn to page 10.

You take a look at the map. She's right—it doesn't look far away. The two of you grab your belongings and start walking.

It is boiling hot. The sun beats down on you. Sweat gathers on your forehead and under your arms. "Boy, I could use a cool glass of lemonade," you say, wiping your face with your hand. Lisa nods. You notice she looks awfully red.

"Are you okay?" you ask, looking at her. "Why don't you drink some water from the canteen?" You hand it to her.

"Thanks," she murmurs. "I'm feeling a bit warm." To your horror, you watch as she tips the canteen back—and only a few drops drip out.

"The canteen!" you shriek in horror. Lisa stares at it. "There's a tiny hole here," she says, feeling around the bottom. "All our water must have leaked out." She grabs your hand. "Don't worry," she whispers. "It's not much far—"

Turn to page 82.

"Tomorrow," Maggie says, looking smug, "Coyote can tell you about the curse of the burial room."

"Curse?" You don't want to wait until morning.

Coyote looks off into the night as if he is listening to something that no one else can hear. Without a word, he gets up and slips off into the darkness.

"There will be plenty of time for more stories tomorrow. In fact, we have all summer. Let's turn in," your uncle says.

As you head for your tent, you pull Maggie aside. "Tell me about the curse," you beg.

"It's like most curses," she says. "Anyone who enters the sacred burial room will die a terrible death."

"Oh, is that all?" you say, trying to make a joke. "I thought it might be something bad."

"Well, there are some gory details, but you'll have to wait until tomorrow. I know how scared you can get." Giggling, she gives your tent flap a pull and heads off into the night.

Turn to page 53.

The Jeep has come to a fork in the road. "You know, I'm not sure which way to go," Lisa says. "This is my first trip to the outpost without Coyote. I think it's left, toward the mesas."

You shake your head. "Well, I came in on that road," you say, pointing to the right fork. "I remember those large cacti."

"I don't think so," Lisa says. "You're probably turned around. It happens in the desert." She frowns. "Well, maybe you are right. Are you sure?"

If you tell her to head toward the cacti, turn to page 63.

If you tell her to head toward the mesas, turn to page 54.

As he reaches the middle of the room, a trapdoor opens above his head. *"Yeowww!"* he screams, as an urn of live scorpions spills out on his head!

For some reason, the scorpions don't touch you or Maggie. They only want Coyote. In horror, you and Maggie watch as the scorpions sting and bite the foiled grave robber.

"Come on. Let's get out of here!" cries Maggie.

"Wait!" you say, shouting above Coyote's screams. A large wooden box has appeared near the door. You don't remember it being there before. Grabbing the box, you and Maggie run out of the room. You retrieve the stone.

"Look, the glow is fading," you say, holding it up.

"We'll never find our way out of here without light!" Maggie cries.

Turn to page 26.

48

Uncle Evan sees how much you want it. "Listen, Coyote. Let them have it for the day. I trust them," he says.

"Fine," says Coyote, slapping the stone into your palm. "Have it your way." He tries to smile but his teeth are clenched.

"Great!" says Maggie. "Let's go!"

You go back to your tent and put on your fanny pack. It holds your compass, first-aid kit, power bars, and an extra bandanna. Maggie gets hers too and fills up a canteen with water. Even though she has always been a pain, you decide that trying to decipher the petroglyphs on the stone with her might be a lot of fun.

"Where should we begin?" you ask once you and Maggie are sitting in your uncle's old trailer, the official site office of the archaeological dig.

Maggie wrinkles her nose. "It's simple," she says in her all-knowing way. "We start with research."

Turn to page 83.

The old man narrows his partially crossed eyes and stares at you. "This ain't no trick is it? If it is," he says, pulling a long, sharp knife from a leather pouch, "my silver beauty will taste your blood."

"It's no trick," you say hastily. "Really!"

He puts the knife away. "Casey McKee, at your service."

McKee! The name clicks in your brain. He's the treasure hunter you heard about. "Help me with Lisa. Please!" you ask again.

Casey carefully picks up Lisa and lays her on the backseat of his cluttered Jeep. "Hop in," he says.

You get in beside him just as he steps on the gas. Giving you a glance he says, "You should never ride with strangers. I know a man who took a ride from a stranger and they found parts of his body in four different states."

"Was it in the newspaper?" you ask.

"No. I just know about it." Casey laughs. "Never pick up hitchhikers neither. No siree. It ain't safe." Suddenly he gives you a look that causes your palms to sweat. "You ain't no hitchhiker, are you?"

Turn to page 29.

"Hey, you know what?" she asks as you drive off.

"What?"

"I forgot to tell you. Tonight we're holding a séance. Coyote is going to try to find out if evil spirits are haunting the camp."

You give a nervous laugh. "You don't really think that's possible, do you?"

Lisa's face grows serious. "Of course I do. And so do several other workers."

You wrap your arms around your chest. Suddenly you're cold. Thankfully, you don't discuss ghosts for the rest of the ride, and before you know it, you're approaching the dig.

"Thanks for the ride, Lisa," you call out, running for your tent.

"Sure. And don't forget about the séance. We'd like you to be there," she says.

Turn to page 41.

"No. Please!" you scream, as arms wrap around your body. They rip off the sleeping bag . . . to reveal Maggie and Uncle Evan and a group of workers!

"Ha ha ha ha!" laughs Maggie, pointing at you. "I knew you'd fall for it. I just knew it!"

Uncle Evan gives a big belly laugh. "A little joke every now and then raises everyone's spirits. Get it? Raises spirits?" he chuckles, ruffling your hair.

You smile weakly. "Sure. Right."

Maggie grabs your hand. "The séance is over. You didn't miss much. But now Lisa's fixing a late-night snack," she says. "Join us. Her fried spiders are delicious!"

The End

"Snakes give me the creeps," Maggie says.

You smile at your cousin's admission of weakness.

"When Nila discovered that Teewah was dead she was filled with sadness. She wound the beautiful ribbons in her hair and returned to the cave where Teewah lay. She kissed him one last time before holding a snake she'd taken from her father's tent to her own heart. When the two warring families found the young couple, it was too late to save Nila. Teewah and Nila's love had been true and their deaths made the families realize the error of their ways.

"They were buried together in a room deep inside a hillside cavern. The families filled the burial room with wonderful treasures to appease the gods for what they had done."

"Were they buried around here?" you ask.

"Maybe. Many treasure hunters believe they were. No one knows for sure since their tribes have long since died out," Lisa tells you. "But the legend of the two lovers and their burial room full of treasures has persisted. Even now there are treasure hunters around."

Turn to page 44.

Inside your tent you have a table and chair, a chest of drawers, and a cot. The kerosene lamp sputters until you get the wick just right. You spend some time arranging your clothes and putting away your books before getting into bed.

The sound of people talking drifts through the desert air and from time to time flashlight beams rake across the outside of your tent. Soon you're fast asleep.

Swish! *What was that?* you think, sitting straight up. There is a rustling sound like wings flapping against the side of your tent. You feel the hair on the back of your neck stiffen, and you hold perfectly still.

There it is again, the sound of wings, and then another sound. You listen. Slowly the zipper on your tent flap opens and a large, humanlike shadow enters.

Your heartbeat is so loud you are sure the ghostly intruder will hear it and come after you. The creature slides through the air until it is standing in front of your chest of drawers. A small beam of light snakes its way over your dresser.

Turn to page 13.

"Let's go left," you say. Lisa heads toward the mesas. Soon you see a few buildings on the horizon.

"That's the outpost," she tells you. "I was sure Coyote came this way when I drove in with him last week."

You pull to a stop outside a stucco and brick building. A few people are standing on a porch outside.

"Hi," says Lisa, nodding. "Hot day."

"It sure is," says a sunburnt man.

You and Lisa go inside. There are all sorts of items to buy. Canteens, army knives, and tents line one wall of shelves. "I'm going to the back. That's where they keep the food," Lisa tells you.

"Okay. I'll look around here," you say.

It's fun to look at all the stuff—it's much better than the camping store you went to at home.

Turn to page 7.

"Hey, I heard about what happened last night," she says. "Don't let it get you down. Why don't you run into town with me this morning? We'll pick up some supplies."

"Are you ready to do some exploring?" Maggie calls over to you. "Or did you get too scared last night?"

You take a sip of cocoa. Maybe a trip into town would be fun. But you'd really like to show off your stone to Maggie—you know she'll be mad she didn't find it first.

If you go into town with Lisa, turn to page 25.

If you stay at the dig with Maggie, turn to page 23.

56

The trail is hot as you hike along. You follow a little-used path toward a dark rock that juts into the air like a camel's hump. Maggie points out the different kinds of cactus that grow in the region. In a schoolteacher voice she says, "This is a saguaro cactus," or "That funny ball of needles over there is a barrel or compass cactus. It stores a lot of water, but the needles are awfully sharp."

You roll your eyes. She's always such a know-it-all.

After hiking for about an hour you leave the base of the mountains and climb to a saddle ridge. Maggie looks at the map while you take a drink of water from the canteen. The water is warm and has a metallic taste, but you are not about to complain. "How much further?" you ask.

"It should be over there," she says, pointing in the direction of a dry, rock-strewn cliff. "But I don't see it."

"Well let's go look anyhow," you say.

"My, aren't you brave," Maggie says.

You shake your head. "Please. Can't we try to get along for one afternoon?"

Turn to page 16.

"I've got to do it," you tell Maggie. "You wait here, and I'll sneak in. Then, if the coast is clear, you run in and join me."

"Mm-mm," Maggie says, shaking her head and pursing her lips. "I always thought you were an idiot—and now you're proving it."

She really makes you mad when she says things like that.

"Fine. But when I come out wearing the jewels from the tomb of Teewah and Nila, don't think I'm letting you take any!"

You stare at the urn. Nothing. You haven't seen the snake since it went back in. Maybe it's sleeping now. It won't even know you went in and out.

Slowly you creep up toward the mouth of the cave. Ten more steps. Nine. Eight. In a few seconds you'll be inside. Your heart is pounding in your chest. You're sure Maggie is biting her nails. You avoid looking at the urn as you pass by it. Bingo! You're in!

You turn to give Maggie the victory signal—and you see her face crumple in fear.

Turn to page 78.

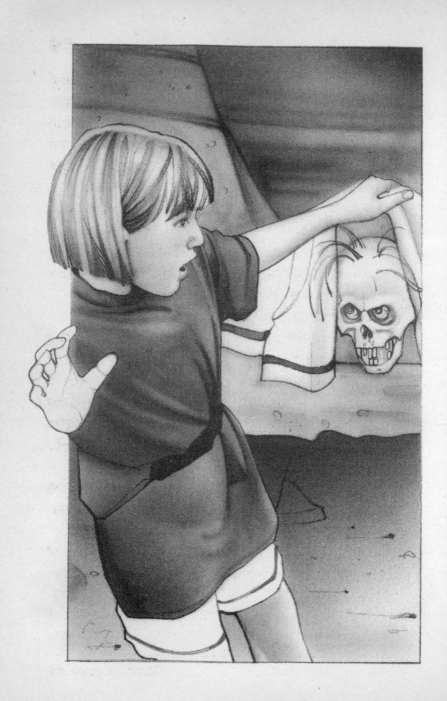

You drop back to where Maggie is standing. "What did Coyote mean, 'or else'?" you ask.

"Or else, legend says a spider woman will come into your house at night, wrap you in a web, and feed you to her children," Maggie answers with a smirk.

"That doesn't really happen!" you say. "Does it?"

Maggie gives you one of her irritating looks. "You're kidding me. It's just a story adults use to keep kids in line."

"Yeah, sure," you agree nervously.

While your uncle gives a lecture on the burial rituals of ancient tribes, you allow your attention to wander. Near you, on the altar, is a blanket. Without thinking, you reach over and gently lift it. A skull grins up at you. Tufts of hair still stick to the top of the head! It gives you the shivers.

As you drop the blanket back in place you see that your act did not go unobserved. Coyote is watching you.

"Would looking at a skeleton be considered disrespectful?" you ask Maggie as you leave the section.

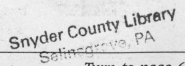

Turn to page 64.

Your hands are shaking so badly you don't know how you're managing to hold on to the stone. "Maggie, this is bad. We've got to get out of here!" Terrified, you move forward, trying to get the image of Casey out of your mind. The cave walls begin to narrow, and you have to walk single file.

"Look at this!" you say as you stumble upon a wall filled with strange markings. You hold the glowing stone close to the wall for Maggie to see.

"Petroglyphs," she breathes.

"See these two here," you say, pointing to two figures lying down, holding snakes.

"Teewah and Nila," Maggie says. "We've found the cave!"

"It also looks like an army of dead people followed them," you say, pointing to a drawing of hundreds of stick figures, carrying bows and spears, marching into the cave.

"Don't say that," she says. "Just don't say things like that."

"Look! The stone!" you say. There's a piece missing in the wall, and your stone fits into it perfectly, like a key. A secret door opens.

Turn to page 79.

"This will stop the blood flow," she tells you.

The pain is incredible, but the tourniquet seems to help. You stare helplessly at Maggie. For once, she's being nice to you.

"I'm going to run back to the dig. My dad has a snakebite antidote there. Just don't move!" she instructs. Her face is streaked with tears. Giving your hand a tiny squeeze, she starts running toward the dig.

You close your eyes. You're almost used to the pain now. You just hope that Maggie runs fast. Before the rattlesnake decides to strike again. . . .

The End

Uncle Evan glances around the room, taking inventory of your few possessions. "I wonder if anything is missing," he says.

"Probably one of your precious books," Maggie says, looking at you.

"May I interrupt?" Coyote steps into the circle of light. "There are those who believe in shape-changers," he says. "Spirits that can take the shape of any animal they wish. Perhaps you have been visited by one."

"Ha!" Maggie says. "My cousin pigged out on beef stew at dinner and it caused a bad dream."

Coyote looks around the tent, then turns and leaves.

Turn to page 8.

"I'm sure I know the way," you say. "Go right. Toward the cacti."

"Okay," says Lisa, turning the Jeep down the road. You drive along, enjoying the barren desert scenery.

"There should be a map in the glove compartment," Lisa tells you. "If you want to double-check."

Just as you find the map, the Jeep begins to jerk, then coughs twice before the motor dies. Black smoke curls up from beneath the hood. Lisa leans forward and taps the circle of glass over the fuel gauge.

"What's wrong?" you ask nervously.

"I don't know. I think we might be out of gas. But the gauge reads full." Lisa gives you a smile. "I'll check. I'm sure it's nothing major."

You wait in the Jeep, nervously fingering the stone.

"Bad news," says Lisa, slamming down the Jeep's hood. "We *are* out of gas. Someone must have tampered with the tank." She pushes a strand of hair off her face. "Well, we might as well start walking. The outpost shouldn't be much farther."

Turn to page 43.

64

Maggie gives you a funny look. "That's number one on the list of things not to do," she says. "Spidey will be visiting you."

"I didn't say I did that," you protest.

"Well if you did," she says, "it will be a short sweet summer—without you." She turns around and runs away.

You try not to think about it. After dinner you head back to your tent. You've been so busy that you've forgotten about your stone. You spend some time reading, trying to figure out the markings on it. Around nine o'clock, Lisa opens your tent flap.

"Hey, you," she says, winking. "Aren't you going to join our séance? Don't be a party pooper."

*If you decide to join them,
turn to page 36.*

*If you stay in your tent and study the stone,
turn to page 40.*

"I have to read these. They could help us!" you tell Maggie. She's not listening to you— she's listening for footsteps instead.

The petroglyphs are familiar—you've seen ones like them before. In minutes, you've cracked the code. The drawings tell you about the wonderful treasure that is to be found, and also the booby traps that are placed around the room.

"Those who understand our language are worthy of life," you say, your finger tracing the pictures.

Suddenly the door to the cave bursts open. You must have left the stone key in the door!

"I knew I'd find you pesky kids in here!" says Coyote, an evil grin on his face. "You should have left the stone with me, like I wanted you to. But no. You had to go snooping around yourselves."

"You've got it all wrong," you say, taking a few steps back.

"Shut up," Coyote snarls. "I've had enough of you and your cousin's mouth." He lunges toward you.

Turn to page 47.

"Hey," a voice booms from behind you. You quickly shove the stone in your pocket. "You're up!" It's Uncle Evan. "We're going to do some more digging. Do you to want to take a peek with us?"

"We're going to look around a little first," Maggie says.

"Suit yourselves," Uncle Evan says. "If you want to join us, we'll be in Section A for most of the morning. Right, Coyote?"

"Right," he says slowly, staring at your pocket. "I think the kids have already found something," he tells your uncle. "They were just about to show me what it was."

You swallow. Something about Coyote gives you the creeps. Should you take out the stone and show it to him and your uncle? Or should you keep quiet, and do some cryptology on your own?

*If you reveal the stone,
turn to page 70.*

*If you keep quiet,
turn to page 24.*

"Please! Over here! Help!" you gasp, flailing your arms in the air. It seems like the more you run, the farther away the person is.

Finally you think he's heard you. "Please. Help me," you gasp. "My friend Lisa . . ." Your words drift off as the figure gets closer.

It's a young man wearing shorts and a tank top, carrying a huge pitcher of water. Gasping, you fall on your knees as he lifts the pitcher to your face.

You part your lips—it's torture to wait any longer for a drink. And then you taste . . . your own sweat. Stricken, your eyes flip open. There is no young man. No pitcher. And no water.

It was a hallucination.

The End

"We've found it! We've found the cave!" Maggie tells you excitedly. "Remember? Nila's tribe were snake people. And Teewah was killed with a rattler. This snake must be guarding the tomb!"

This could make you famous! You could write a book about it—and speak about your discovery at fancy dinners. "We've got to go in," you tell Maggie, forgetting your fear of caves. "It's the chance of a lifetime!"

Maggie shakes her head. "I don't think that's such a good idea. What if we get bit? That is some serious rattler. We can always come back here with my dad and his crew."

You shake your head. "No. Coyote was already on to us. What if he followed us—and claims the treasure for himself?" At that thought, the two of you quickly glance around. There is no one in sight.

"Well, it's up to you," Maggie says. "No way nohow am I going in there."

If you decide to risk going into the cave, turn to page 57.

If you think you should go back to the dig, turn to page 81.

When you open the door to the trailer the blast of air-conditioned air is shocking. Uncle Evan is talking with two of the workers, his face taut with worry.

"Thank goodness you're back. You were gone so long, I was starting to organize a search!" he says, wrapping the two of you in a bear hug.

After you've showered and changed, you find Uncle Evan and Maggie waiting for you at the dining tent. Maggie is gulping down chili when you arrive.

You point to the large box. "We found this in a cave in the mountains," you tell him.

"I know. And Maggie told me about Casey and Coyote. I can't believe Coyote was so greedy," he says. "I guess the scorpions took all the bite out of him."

"Now that Dumbo is here, can we open the box?" Maggie asks. You knew her niceness in the cave was too good to last.

Turn to page 85.

Uncle Evan sits down beside you. "What do you have there?"

"A stone I found," you say, taking it out of your pocket.

"Could I take a look at it?" asks Coyote, holding out his hand.

"We're trying to figure out what the pictures mean," Maggie volunteers. "I think the stone is a real artifact."

Coyote studies the stone for several minutes. "This stone is authentic. You should not be carrying it around in your pocket. I'll take care of it for you." He starts to put the stone into a small pouch on his belt.

"Hey!" The strength in your voice surprises you. "Give that back. It's mine."

Coyote seems nervous. "It must be catalogued, numbered, and dated like all the artifacts we unearth."

"Coyote's right, kids," Uncle Evan says.

"But I found it," you insist. "I promise I won't lose it. Please let me hold on to it. Just for today."

Turn to page 48.

"Yes, I'm afraid so," he says. "But the book is very old, and very valuable. I'd say the two of you have done all right for yourselves." Your uncle stands. "I'll lock the book in the safe until we can get it over to the rare books library in Phoenix. After you're finished eating, you two should get some rest."

While Maggie goes back for seconds you pick up the box and look inside. The bottom seems to be loose. Using a knife, you pry up a small piece of wood.

"What are you doing?" Maggie asks, running back.

"There's a false bottom in this box!" you tell her excitedly.

Together, the two of you lift the bottom up. Underneath lie the most beautiful pair of silver bracelets you have ever seen in your life.

The End

You can't wait until this is over. You're hungry all of a sudden. And you're eager to get back to your books and stone.

Again, everyone raises their arms.

"Please, O Great Spirit. Bring peace to our camp," chants Coyote. "Please fill our dig with only happy spirits." He then tells you all to hold hands again. Forcing yourself to play along, you take Maggie's hand. It is as cold as ice. You try to pull your hand away, but she won't let go. That figures. She's such a stickler for rules.

"Hey," you whisper, "you're like an ice cube." You open one eye to look at her. But it's not Maggie! It's a young Native American brave, dressed in traditional clothes. Your mouth drops open in surprise.

He points to his chest, where you see the fang marks of a rattlesnake. Teewah! Giving you a wink, he then points to Coyote and rolls his eyes.

"Does he really think a séance will work?" he breathes in your ear.

The End

74

When they've gone you light your lamp. You want to make sure you're alone. Some of your things on the chest look out of place. But nothing's missing. You walk over to make sure the tent flap is secure. Now you see it—a small stone with markings on the floor. It wasn't there when you went to bed. The stone is smooth to the touch and cool in your hand.

The drawings scratched on the surface are small, but you can make out the figures of a man and a woman. The man seems to be dancing. He holds one hand over his head. The woman has something draped over her shoulders. Is it a snake?

You can't believe what you've found! You really want to take out your hieroglyphic book and do some research, but it is almost four in the morning. So you put the rock under your pillow for safekeeping and turn off the light.

About four hours later, the smell of bacon tugs you from sleep. In the mess tent a few early risers are sitting around holding steaming mugs of coffee. Lisa and Coyote are sitting together, but she hops up to get you a big mug of cocoa.

Turn to page 55.

You grab Maggie's arm. "Do you think this is it? The cave of Teewah and Nila?" you ask. "Maybe the bones are from some unlucky person who went inside. Ghost Dancer got them!"

Maggie shakes off your hand. "Get real. Probably someone just died of heat exhaustion, or . . . *Ahhhhh!*"

Maggie's scream terrifies you, and you almost fall over with fear. She's pointing to the ceramic urn. A gigantic rattlesnake has slithered up from inside. Its head is reared, and its snake eyes are focused on your neck.

"S-S-Snake," Maggie stammers. "D-D-Don't move."

"I won't," you breathe. Your heart is beating double-time. You don't know whether to take your eyes off the snake or not. Maybe staring at it is making it angry.

The snake doesn't look like it's going to attack now. With a soft hiss, it slithers back into the urn. You and Maggie each move back about ten feet.

Turn to page 68.

There in the cave is a fierce warrior, his skull adorned with a cluster of eagle feathers. Behind him stands a tribe of skeleton warriors. "I am Ghost Dancer," he says, planting a spear into the ground. "Protector of Teewah and Nila."

You and Maggie slowly back away from the entrance.

"You two have completed the cycle. Our work is done." He points a bony finger at you. Instinctively you know what he wants. Reaching into your pocket, you take out the stone and toss it into the cave entrance.

"You may keep the box," he says. In a rush of heat and air, he vanishes. A loud explosion almost deafens you. Lightning has struck the entrance of the cave, not more than ten feet away, sealing it forever.

"No one will believe this," Maggie murmurs.

"Let's find our way back," you say. "Uncle Evan will be worried."

After two and a half hours of hard hiking you crest the hill and see the archaeological site at the base of the mountain.

Turn to page 69.

You swallow your pride. "Maggie!" you shout, making your way back out of the cave. "Come on. I wish you would join me. Just lay off the cave jokes, okay?"

Sunlight streams in through the mouth of the cave as you exit. Maggie looks at you, her fingers on her lips.

"Shhh! It's Coyote!" she says, gesturing down the mountain. "I heard something, silly. That's why I stopped. I wanted to find out what it was. He must have followed us!"

Your eyes widen in fear. "He's after the treasure too!"

"C'mon!" Maggie says, pulling you into the cave. She's yanking you down one tunnel after the other.

"Wait a minute!" you say, twisting your arm free. "I think I know the way to go." You pull out your stone. It's glowing.

"This is nice. Just the two of us standing around watching our rock glow," Maggie says. She's trying to be funny but you can hear the fear in her voice.

Turn to page 34.

"Watch out!" she shrieks. In a flash, the snake slithers out of the urn and lunges for your leg. You hear the deadly rattle. It makes you sick to your stomach.

"Owwwwwww!" you cry, as the fangs sink into your leg. Blood spurts down your leg onto your new hiking boots. You grip your calf and sink to the ground, not caring if you land on top of the snake. That's how bad the pain is.

But now that the snake has bit you, it's gone back into the urn.

"Come on!" shouts Maggie, half crying. She runs over and grabs your arm, dragging you backward. Pushing you down, she lifts your leg and begins to suck out the blood with her mouth.

It hurts so much, you want to die.

"This sucks," says Maggie, spitting out a mouthful of blood and venom. "But it's the only way to get out the poison!" After a few minutes she stops and makes a tourniquet from her bandanna.

Turn to page 61.

"Wait. I don't want to go in. I want to go back to my dad!" Maggie says.

Just then you hear footsteps pounding down an adjacent tunnel.

"There's no time!" you say, darting in. "Hurry!"

Ahead of you, in the distance, is a shimmering glow. "There's light up ahead," you say. "Maybe it's another way out of the cave. Come on."

Maggie holds on to your T-shirt as you approach the light. Then you're in a room where the light seems to be coming from the walls. The door shuts.

"Look!" Maggie pulls your arm so hard you spin around. The room is carved out of the rock underbelly of the mountain. A series of racks lines the walls.

There are shapes on the racks covered in blankets. Scattered around the cave are bowls filled with dried flowers, small painted clay pots, beaded necklaces and rings, and primitive weapons.

Turn to page 14.

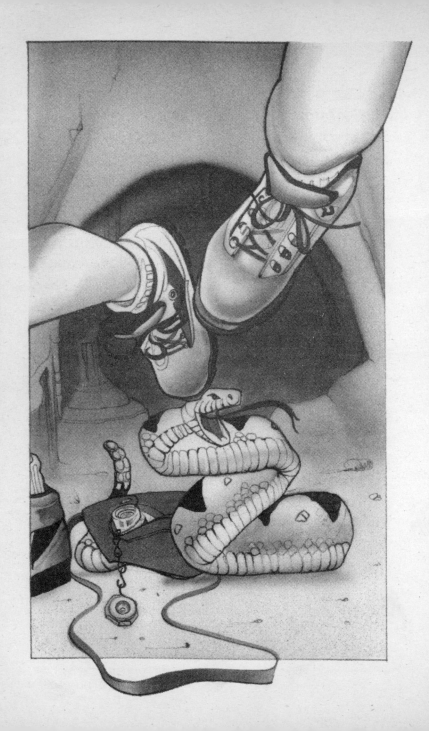

"I guess you're right," you say dejectedly. "If Coyote gets here, then he gets here." Sighing, you take one last, longing look at the cave, then head back toward the dig.

Maggie begins to whistle. "I knew you would be too scared to go in," she says between whistles. "That's so typical of you. Besides, we don't even know if that is the treasure. It might just be a regular old cave."

"Stop whistling," you say irritably. Despite what she says, you can tell she's secretly relieved. You know how scared she is of snakes. You're just about to torture her with a scary snake story when you hear a noise. It sounds like . . . like a rattle.

Turning, you see that the snake has come out of the urn, and its large, meaty body is slipping and sliding over the desert floor, heading straight for you.

"Run!" you scream, sprinting off. Maggie is right at your heels. Or is it the snake?

The End

82

You gasp as Lisa's hand slips out of yours and she collapses onto the ground. Heatstroke!

"Lisa! Lisa!" you say, slapping her face. You can't believe this is happening. You take off your bandanna and wipe it across her brow. Looking up, you see three vultures circling in the blazing sunlight.

You have to do something. Should you stay with Lisa or try to find help?

If you decide to go for help,
turn to page 18.

If you decide to stay and wait,
turn to page 9.

The office is full of books about the White Mountains and the Apache tribes that once lived in this part of Arizona. "There seem to be a lot of stories about ghosts in these books," you say, looking up from a picture of an angel-like apparition floating above the earth.

"Of course there are," Maggie says. "Native Americans have always believed in the spirit world." She doesn't say *Stupid,* but you can hear it in her voice. After an hour or so of searching through dusty old books, you decide you're ready to go.

The sun shines brightly in the late morning sky as you and Maggie reach the mountain. The stone silhouettes seem to dance along the ridge of the hill in the shifting shadows of clouds scudding past. Something darts across the path in front of you; all you see is the flash of an eye glinting in the dazzling light.

"Oh!" you say, jumping back.

Maggie gives you a little push. "Please," she drawls. "Don't tell me you're afraid of caves and lizards. You really should pick another place to vacation in besides the desert."

Turn to page 32.

84

You press yourself against the hard rock wall and move slowly along. It's pretty dark; you can't see well at all.

"Yes, here I am, on my way to becoming rich and famous!" you shout. Your voice echoes throughout the cave.

You thought Maggie would be right behind you. Knowing her, she's probably getting ready to scare you. Then you realize that not only does she now have the map, she has the canteen. Maybe you acted too fast. Maybe you should go back and get her.

If you decide to continue on your own,
turn to page 30.

If you go back and get Maggie,
turn to page 77.

"Your cousin is far from dumb," says your uncle. "And yes, why don't you open the box." He gathers the rest of the workers around you. Carefully, he pries off the top of the box. Inside is a small book covered in some kind of animal skin. Uncle Evan opens the book. "It's written in an old dialect, but I think I can decipher it," he says.

After turning the last page, he puts the book down.

"What is it?" you want to know.

"It's the diary of a great warrior, known as Ghost Dancer. It tells how the families of Teewah and Nila fought over a sacred stone, each believing the other family had stolen it. This was why Teewah and Nila had to meet secretly. The stone was never found. It also says that one day the chosen ones will return the stone, and when that happens the ghosts of Teewah and Nila will finally be able to rest."

"That's it?" Maggie says.

Turn to page 71.

"I can't breathe!" you whisper, taking little gulps of air. Memories of last year flash in your head. Tears run down your face. Your hands still clutch the stone. It's shining brighter than ever.

Last summer, they found you. It took a man with a special power chisel to chip away part of the cave to free you. Afterward you were treated at the hospital. But when you went home you had nightmares about the cave. You would wake up crying in the middle of the night, trying to catch your breath. Ever since that experience any small space has made you feel uncomfortable.

And now here you are again.

"Maggie!" you scream. *"Help me! I'm stuck!"* But you're so deep in the cave, you don't think she'll ever hear you.

Why did I leave her? you think. It seems impossible, but it's for real. Your worst fears have come true. You're trapped in a cave again. And this time there's no way out.

The End

You might as well try to go along with it. It's easy to concentrate on Coyote's words—the night is so quiet. At first your ears pick up every sound. But soon you're used to being outside, holding hands in a circle. In unison, you repeat Coyote's words with the others. They make no sense to you. But before you know it, you are in a deep spell.

How did this happen? you think. Your mind knows what is going on, but your body won't move. It's as if your brain can't communicate with your body.

"Good!" says a female voice. "They're under!" You force your eyes to open just a little. You see that Lisa has broken free from the circle and joined Coyote in the middle.

"Yes! We don't have much time. We've got to get the stone from that pesky kid's tent and find the cave before Evan gets back," Coyote says. Even though he's speaking loudly, no one moves.

"And then the treasure will be ours!" Lisa says.

Helplessly you watch as the two of them run toward your tent. Will Uncle Evan get back in time?

The End